Sleeping Beauty

by Louise John
and Natascia Ugliano

Evans

First published 2007
Evans Brothers Limited
2A Portman Mansions
Chiltern St
London W1U 6NR

British Library Cataloguing in Publication Data

John, Louise
    Sleeping Beauty. - (Skylarks)
    1. Sleeping Beauty (Tale) - Juvenile fiction 2. Fairy tales
    3. Children's stories
    I. Title II. Ugliano, Natascia
    823.9'2[J]

ISBN-13: 9780237533861 (hb)
ISBN-13: 9780237534042 (pb)
Printed in China by WKT Co. Ltd

Series Editor: Louise John
Design: Robert Walster
Production: Jenny Mulvanny

Contents

Chapter One   7

Chapter Two   13

Chapter Three   18

Chapter Four   22

Chapter Five   28

Chapter Six   31

Chapter Seven   35

Chapter Eight   43

Chapter One

Once upon a time, in a land far away, there was a king and a queen. They lived together in a beautiful palace and life was good. The only thing that made the king and queen sad was that they had no children. Many years went by and when the queen finally gave birth to a baby girl, everyone in the kingdom was delighted.

The king and queen held a christening to celebrate. They invited the seven good fairies of the land to be the baby's godmothers and each fairy was to give the baby a magical gift. But, on the day of the christening, an extra fairy arrived.

This fairy was ugly and old. The king
and queen hadn't invited her because
they hadn't seen her for a long time and
thought she was dead. The fairy was
very cross indeed.

Soon the time came for the fairies to
give the baby princess their gifts. The
first said she would be beautiful, the

second said she would be clever, one
fairy said she would be graceful, another
gave her the gift of dance. The fifth and
sixth fairies gave her the gift of music,

so she would sing and play like an angel. The seventh fairy held back. She was feeling worried about what the angry old fairy was going to do.

The old fairy pushed forwards and pointed her wand at the princess's crib.

"The princess will prick her finger on a spinning wheel and die!" she spat, glaring at the baby. Everyone gasped in horror and the queen began to cry.

The seventh good fairy stepped forward quickly. She wasn't powerful enough to undo the curse, but she could help a little.

"Here is my gift," she said. "The princess will not die. She will prick her finger and fall asleep for a hundred years. At the end of that time, she will be awoken by the kiss of a prince."

The king and queen were relieved but they ordered all the spinning wheels in the kingdom to be destroyed right away, just in case.

Chapter Two

Sixteen years passed and the princess grew up into a lovely young girl, just as the fairies had promised. Then one day, when she was exploring an old part of the castle she hadn't seen before, she came across a little room in one of the towers. Inside, an old woman sat spinning some thread.

The woman didn't know about the king's order and smiled at the princess.

"Hello, my dear, would you like to spin some thread with me?" she asked.

"Oh, yes," replied the princess, who was feeling a little lonely and bored.

But, as soon as the princess's hand touched the spindle, she pricked her finger and fell to the floor in a deep, deep sleep. The old woman cried for help straight away and soon the room was full of people, all trying to wake the princess up. They tried everything, but the princess could not be woken. Just as the seventh fairy had said, the princess had fallen into the deepest and longest of sleeps.

The king and queen moved the sleeping princess to the royal chamber and placed her on a bed with silken covers. They watched over her day and

night and cried for their beautiful
daughter. She slept so deeply
and peacefully and the king
and queen knew she
would sleep on for a
hundred years until
the spell could be
broken.

Chapter Three

The good fairy who had helped to save the princess's life was far away, but she heard what had happened and came to the palace straight away. She knew that when the princess woke up in a hundred years time, she would know no one and be sad and lonely. All the people she would remember from before her sleep would be dead. There was only one thing for her to do.

The fairy walked around the palace and touched every

living thing with her wand, casting a
spell as she went. Everyone in the castle,
the guards, the maids, the cooks and
even the princess's dog, all fell into a
deep sleep. They would sleep for a
hundred years and wake up when the
princess woke up. The king and queen

did not want to be part of this spell and they stayed awake so that they could watch over their sleeping child as long as they could.

Then the fairy made tall trees and twisting sharp brambles grow high up around the castle, until it was almost completely hidden. Only the very tops of the tallest towers could be seen.

The seasons changed and years went by, and no one came near the castle.

Chapter Four

And so a hundred years passed. One day, a prince was out riding near the palace and saw the castle towers rising out of the dark, thick wood. He asked some of the local people about it.

"It's a haunted castle!" said one.

"The place is bewitched!" said another.

Then, finally, he was told the real story of Sleeping Beauty by an

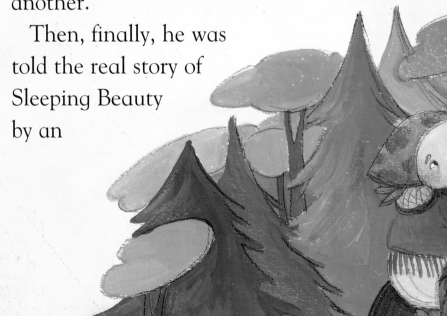

old woman. He decided that if
the sleeping princess needed a
prince to rescue her, he was
the man for the job!

"Many princes have died
trying to break through

those thorns," warned the old woman.

But the prince was determined and set off towards the mysterious and overgrown palace.

To the prince's surprise, the thorny brambles were easy to pass through. They almost seemed to move out of his way! When he looked back he saw that the plants had closed behind him again, so no one could follow. He reached the castle door and went inside. He could not believe his eyes! There were sleeping people and animals everywhere! They were lying on the floor or standing up.

They were sitting down at the table to eat, with their plates still full of food and their cups still full of drink. At last, he came to a room with a bed in it. And lying on the bed was the most beautiful princess he had ever seen.

The prince knelt by the bed and kissed her rosebud lips. The evil spell was broken and the princess opened her eyes and smiled.

"Is it you, my prince?" she said.

Chapter Five

Now that the spell was broken,
everyone else began to wake up, too,
and the palace started to come back to
life. The princess was hungry after such
a long sleep and a great feast was
cooked. Musicians played music that
had not been heard for the last
hundred years and everyone danced in
the great hall.

The princess was so pleased to be
awake and told the prince all about the
lovely dreams the good fairy had given
her when she was asleep. In those
dreams, the princess had seen the
prince and knew he was coming.

They talked and talked and slowly fell
more and more in love.

After the feast, the princess and the

prince were married in the palace
chapel and lived happily ever after…
   Or did they?

Chapter Six

The next morning the prince left the palace and went home to his mother and father, the king and queen of another kingdom. They were worried and asked why he had not come home the night before. The prince said he had got lost riding in the forest. He had taken shelter at a kind old man's house.

The king thought this was the truth, but the queen did not believe her son. The prince was away more and more and was spending many days at a time away from home. She did not trust him at all and began to wonder if he had got married without telling her.

The prince lived like this for two years and the prince and the princess were very happy together.

They had two children. First of all, a

little girl, whose name was Sun and then a little boy, whose name was Moon. They all lived together in the princess's palace.

Before his visits away, the prince's mother always asked him where he was going, but the prince was too frightened to tell the truth about his new family. His mother was an ogress from the Land of Ogres and she was a terrifying woman. It was often said that she liked to eat the odd child or two (as ogres do). So, the prince kept his new wife and Sun and Moon a secret.

Two years later, the prince's father died and the prince became king in his place. This meant that the princess was now queen.

The new king told everyone about his

secret wedding and brought his queen
and his children back to the palace in a
great ceremony. His mother, the ogress,
was furious.

Chapter Seven

Unfortunately, soon afterwards, the new king had to go away to war. Foolishly, he left his mother in charge of the kingdom and asked her to look after his wife and children. As soon as the king had gone, his mother sent the queen and the children away to live in a house in the woods. The ogress was definitely planning something.

A few days later, she arrived at the house and said to the butler:

"I'm feeling very hungry. I think I'd like to eat little Sun today."

The butler was very shocked, even though he knew she was an ogress.

"No, Madam!"

"Yes, that is what I want. I'd like you to cook her for me in a nice sauce," replied the ogress.

The butler was afraid but he knew he could not kill Sun. She was beautiful and sweet and just a little girl. He tried to think of a plan. He went to the fields and killed a lamb and cooked it with a tasty mint sauce.

The ogress thought the meal was very tasty indeed and as she was greedily eating, the butler quickly took Sun to his own mother's house in the woods to hide her.

The next day, the ogress said:

"I so enjoyed my delicious meal yesterday. Today I would like to eat Moon. Maybe I could try him in a cheese sauce?"

The butler was horrified but he knew what to do this time. He took Moon to join his big sister in the woods and then quickly killed a goat, which he cooked with his best cheese sauce.

"Scrumptious!" said the ogress. "What a fine cook you are. Tomorrow I think I will eat the new queen with another of your lovely sauces."

This time the butler didn't know what to do. He didn't think he could fool the ogress again. He took a knife to the new queen's room and told her what he had come to do.

"Kill me then," said the queen. "I don't want to live without my children!"

Both the butler and the queen began to cry.

"Come quickly," said the butler, "and I will take you to your children. They are alive and well in the forest."

When the ogress didn't get her dinner on time she began to wonder what had happened.

She looked all over the palace for the butler and couldn't find him. Then she started to look outside in the palace grounds. Suddenly, she heard the sound of children singing and her mouth began to water.

She followed the sound of the voices
into the woods and soon came across
the queen playing with her children in
the butler's mother's house. The ogress
flew into a rage, and the queen wept.

Chapter Eight

The next day, the ogress asked for a large cauldron to be put in the palace courtyard. She began to fill it with toads, poisonous snakes, spiders and all sorts of horrible creatures. Then she ordered that the butler, the queen and the children be brought to her with their hands tied behind their backs. The ogress was just about to throw them all into the cauldron when the king unexpectedly arrived back from war! He was horrified and demanded to know what on earth she was doing.

The ogress was shocked. She hadn't thought she would get caught out.

She had been going to tell her son
that his wife and children had been
eaten by wolves. In shame, she jumped
into the cauldron and was eaten
straight away by all the horrible
creatures she had put in there!

44

The king promised never to leave his wife and children's side again and, this time, they all did live happily ever after.

If you enjoyed this story, why not read another *Skylarks* book?

Awkward Annie

by Julia Williams and Tim Archbold

How would you like it if people thought you were awkward? Awkward Annie – that's what Mum and Dad call me. I don't think I'm awkward. Not really.

They soon had to change their minds though on the day that Awful Aunt Aggie took us to the park, didn't they? Brave Bella they call me now.

Well, someone had to save the day…

Hurricane Season
by David Orme and Doreen Lang

Grace and her family had come to
Florida on holiday to visit Grandma and
Grandpa. Mum and Dad were staying
in a hotel on Palm Beach but Grace
wanted to stay in Grandma and
Grandpa's trailer. She hadn't been
there long when the weather started
to change. There was going to be
a hurricane and it was going to be
a big one!

Skylarks titles include:

Awkward Annie
by Julia Williams and Tim Archbold
HB 9780237533847
PB 9780237534028

Sleeping Beauty
by Louise John and Natascia Ugliano
HB 9780237533861
PB 9780237534042

Detective Derek
by Karen Wallace and Beccy Blake
HB 9780237533885
PB 9780237534066

Hurricane Season
by David Orme and Doreen Lang
HB 9780237533892
PB 9780237534073

Spiggy Red
by Penny Dolan and Cinzia Battistel
HB 9780237533854
PB 9780237534035

London's Burning
by Pauline Francis and Alessandro Baldanzi
HB 9780237533878
PB 9780237534059